A NOTE TO PARENTS

When your children are ready to "step into reading," giving them the right books—and lots of them—is as crucial as giving them the right food to eat. **Step into Reading Books** present exciting stories and information reinforced with lively, colorful illustrations that make learning to read fun, satisfying, and worthwhile. They are priced so that acquiring an entire library of them is affordable. And they are beginning readers with an important difference—they're written on four levels.

Step 1 Books, with their very large type and extremely simple vocabulary, have been created for the very youngest readers. **Step 2 Books** are both longer and slightly more difficult. **Step 3 Books,** written to mid-second-grade reading levels, are for the child who has acquired even greater reading skills. **Step 4 Books** offer exciting nonfiction for the increasingly proficient reader.

Children develop at different ages. **Step into Reading Books,** with their four levels of reading, are designed to help children become good—and interested—readers *faster.* The grade levels assigned to the four steps—preschool through grade 1 for Step 1, grades 1 through 3 for Step 2, grades 2 and 3 for Step 3, and grades 2 through 4 for Step 4—are intended only as guides. Some children move through all four steps very rapidly; others climb the steps over a period of several years. These books will help your child "step into reading" in style!

Library of Congress Cataloging-in-Publication Data
Wheeler, Cindy. Bookstore cat / Cindy Wheeler. p. cm. — (Step into reading. Step 1 book)
SUMMARY: Mulligan, the bookstore cat, has an exciting day when a pigeon wanders into the store.
ISBN 0-394-84109-3 (trade) — ISBN 0-394-94109-8 (lib. bdg.)
[1. Cats—Fiction. 2. Bookstores—Fiction.] I. Title. II. Title: Bookstore cat.
III. Series. PZ7. W5593Bo 1994 [E]—dc20 89-42635

Manufactured in the United States of America   10 9 8 7 6

STEP INTO READING is a trademark of Random House, Inc.

Random House, Inc. New York, Toronto, London, Sydney, Auckland

Step into Reading™

Bookstore Cat

By Cindy Wheeler

A Step 1 Book

Random House 🏠 New York

This is Mulligan.

Mulligan is

a working cat.

He works in a bookstore.

His jobs
are...

doorman,

mouse-catcher,

watchcat,

and
baby-sitter.

7

Mulligan is
also great at
picking out
books...

...and entertaining

customers!

One day, the bookseller
made a new sign
for the window.

Mulligan was curious
about the new sign.

STORY HOUR
TODAY

He kept
an eye on it
all morning.

Soon the bookstore
was very busy.

But Mulligan
didn't notice.
He had just spotted
a pigeon.

In the bookstore,
everyone was watching
a show.

In the bookstore window,
Mulligan was watching
the pigeon.

Just then a customer
came in.

Right behind her
came the pigeon.
No one noticed.
No one except
Mulligan, that is!
"NO BIRDS
IN THE STORE!"
meowed Mulligan.

But the pigeon
didn't leave.
"Okay," thought Mulligan.
"Time to get to work!"

Mulligan sprang

into action.

So did the pigeon.

The pigeon landed right
next to a funny-looking
green bird.

"Oh, no!"
Mulligan thought.
"Now there are TWO
birds in the bookstore!"

Mulligan did what
any bookstore cat
would do.

He pounced!

Feathers flew!

Books fell!

People ran!

When all
was quiet...

...Mulligan had one bird.
The bookseller
had the other.

"Well done,"
purred Mulligan.

Every bookstore
needs a bookstore cat,
don't you think?